PLEASE PLAY SAFE!

Penguin's Guide to Playground Safety

by MARGERY CUYLER

Illustrated by

WILL HILLENBRAND

SCHOLASTIC PRESS * NEW YORK

TO MYLES WHO SMILES
—M.C.

TO ALEXA AND ADRIENNE,
MANY HAPPY PLAY DAYS
—W.H.

When friends go to the playground with Penguin,
they should run so fast that they knock each other down.

WATCH OUT!

Is that right?

No, that's wrong.
When friends go to the playground with Penguin,
they should walk, not run, so no one gets hurt.
THAT'S MORE LIKE IT!

When Elephant plays on the seesaw,
he should jump off quickly so that
his friend bumps to the ground.

THUD!

Is that right?

No, that's wrong.
When Elephant plays on the seesaw,
he should stay put until his friend climbs off.
EASY DOES IT!

When Chimpanzee plays on the monkey bars,
she should grab the rungs
before her friend makes it across.

HERE I COME!

Is that right?

No, that's wrong.
When Chimpanzee plays on the monkey bars,
she should wait until her friend reaches the other side.
WHEE!

When Bear wants to play on the slide,
she should crawl up the front while her
friend slides down.

LOOK AT ME!

Is that right?

No, that's wrong.

When Bear wants to play on the slide,
she should climb up the ladder
and wait her turn.

I'M NEXT!

When Hippo wants to play catch with her friend,
she should throw the ball at his head.

BOINK!

Is that right?

No, that's wrong.
When Hippo wants to play catch with her friend,
she should toss the ball when he is ready.

GREAT CATCH!

When Pig rides his scooter, he should throw
his helmet on the ground before he sets off.

HERE GOES!

Is that right?

No, that's wrong.
When Pig rides his scooter,
he should wear his helmet in case he has an accident.
WHOOPS! I'M ALL RIGHT.

When Rhino plays in the sandbox with his friend,
he should kick sand in his face.

KICK! KICK!

Is that right?

No, that's wrong.
When Rhino plays in the sandbox,
he should ask his friend to help him dig.
SCOOP! SCOOP!

When Parrot plays tag, she should fly
into her friend's face so that she can't see.

FLAP! FLAP!

Is that right?

No, that's wrong.
When Parrot plays tag, she should
tap her friend gently on the back.
YOU'RE IT!

When Giraffe wants to
play with her jump rope,
she should use it to trip her friend.
GOTCHA!

Is that right?

No, that's wrong.
When Giraffe wants to play
with her jump rope,
she should turn
the rope and skip.
HIP HOP!

When Lion wants to play
on the swing,
he should run behind his friend
and get knocked over.
KAPOW!

Is that right?

No, that's wrong.
When Lion wants to play on the swing,
he should wait until his friend
stops and gets off.
YIPPEE! MY TURN!

When it's time for friends to go home,
they should leave their playthings behind.
GOTTA GO!
Is that right?

No, that's wrong.
When it's time for friends to go home,
they should take their playthings with them.
BYE-BYE!

LET'S PLAY AGAIN SOON!